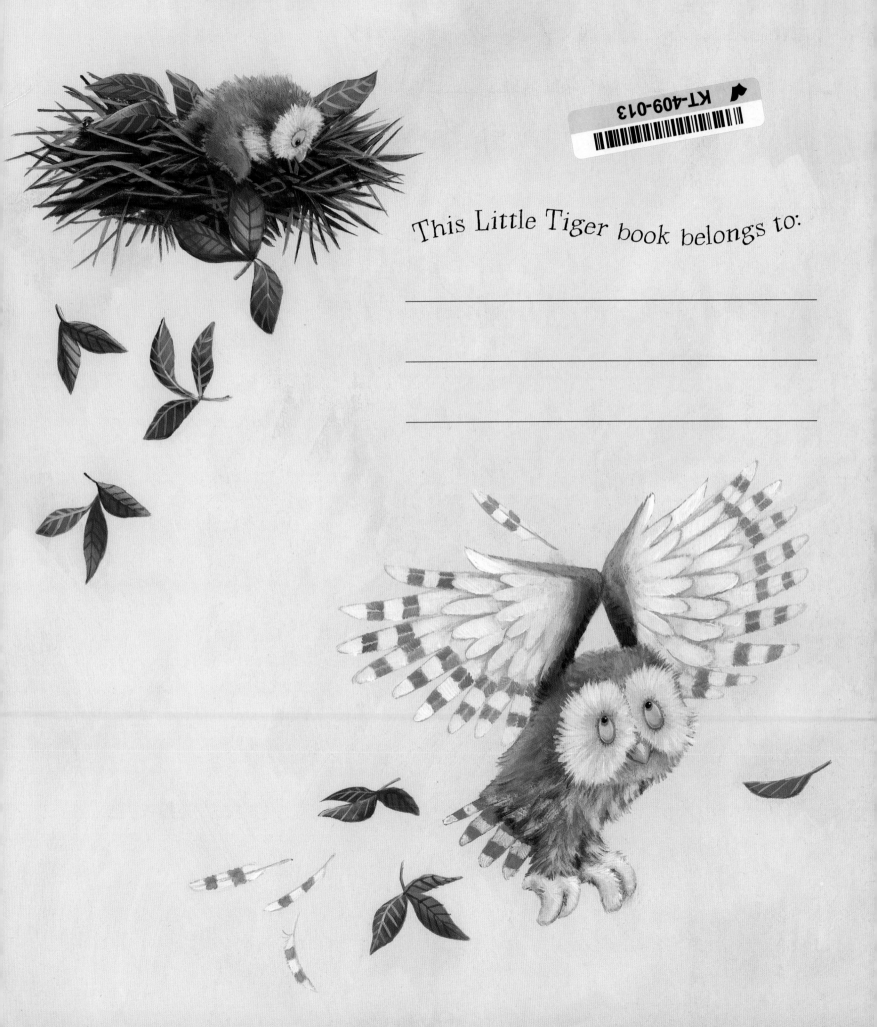

This Little Tiger book belongs to:

_____

_____

_____

For Maxine and Chris – J C

LITTLE TIGER PRESS LTD,
an imprint of the Little Tiger Group
1 Coda Studios
189 Munster Road, London SW6 6AW
www.littletiger.co.uk

First published in Great Britain 2012
This edition published 2018
Text and illustrations copyright © Jane Chapman 2012
Visit Jane Chapman at www.ChapmanandWarnes.com
Jane Chapman has asserted her right to be identified
as the author and illustrator of this work under
the Copyright, Designs and Patents Act, 1988
A CIP catalogue record for this book is available
from the British Library • All rights reserved

ISBN 978-1-78881-030-2
LTP/2700/2946/0719
Printed in China
4 6 8 10 9 7 5 3

CD contains:
1 - complete story with original
music and sound effects
2 - story with page turn pings to encourage
learner readers to join in

Running time over 15 mins
Music composed by Mark Bates
Story read by Anna Crace
This recording copyright
© Little Tiger Press Ltd 2018
℗ Mark Bates

All rights of the producer and owner of the
recorded work reserved. Unauthorised public
performance, broadcasting, copying and hiring
of this recording prohibited.

I'M NOT SLEEPY!

Jane Chapman

LITTLE TIGER

LONDON

At bedtime, Grandma always carried Mo up to the top of the tree.

"It's a long way up for a little owlet," she puffed.

Hop... Jump... Flutter...

FLUMP!

"Ooof," she huffed,
sliding him down.
"Here we are!"

Grandma smoothed soft leaves
into a cosy nest, and sat Mo
carefully in the middle.

"Play with me?" giggled Mo.

"No, Sweetie, it's time
for bed," smiled Grandma.
And she blew him a kiss,
and hopped down to
her book.

The stars were fading when
Grandma heard a rustle.
"Is that you, Mo?"
"Yes! . . . And I haven't had
my Bedtime Biscuit!"

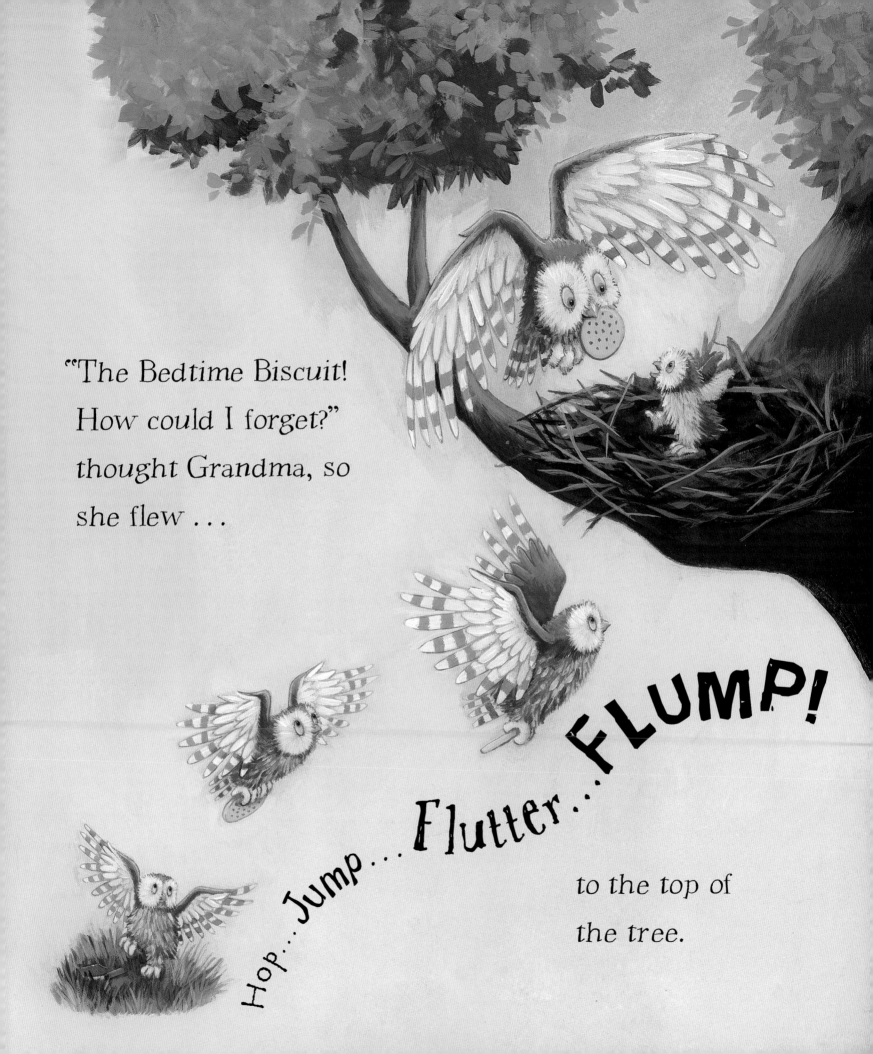

"The Bedtime Biscuit! How could I forget?" thought Grandma, so she flew ...

Hop... Jump... Flutter... **FLUMP!**

to the top of the tree.

Grandma sat and waited for the Bedtime Biscuit to be finished.

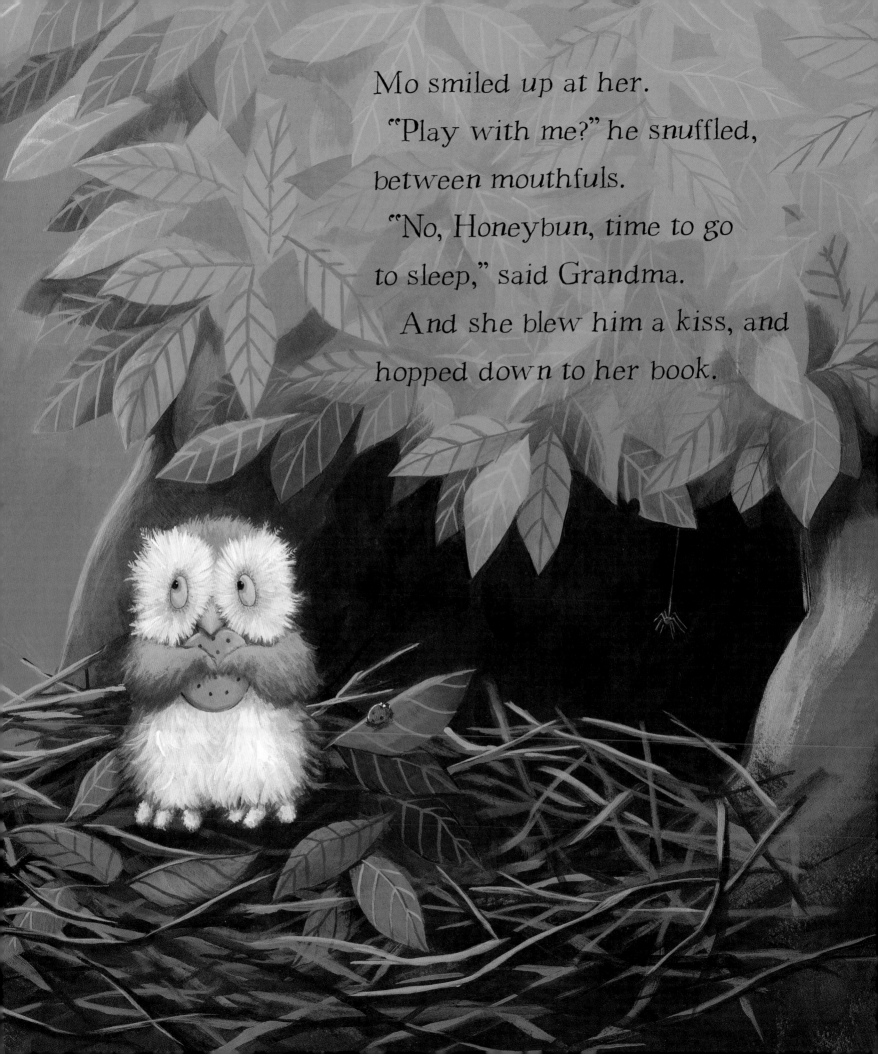

Mo smiled up at her.

"Play with me?" he snuffled,
between mouthfuls.

"No, Honeybun, time to go
to sleep," said Grandma.

And she blew him a kiss, and
hopped down to her book.

The last bats were going home when leaves began to rain down from above. "Mo," Grandma called, "is everything all right?"

"No! ... And I'm not tucked in!"

"He's not tucked in!" sighed Grandma. "Up we go."

Hop ... Jump ... Flutter ... **FLUMP!**

...right to the top of the tree.

Grandma plumped and prodded...

and tucked and rolled ...

until Mo looked like a
wriggly, green pancake.

"Play with me?" he laughed.

"No, Pickle, it's BEDTIME," said Grandma.

"No more noise now . . . unless there's an Emergency." And she blew him a kiss, and hopped down to her book.

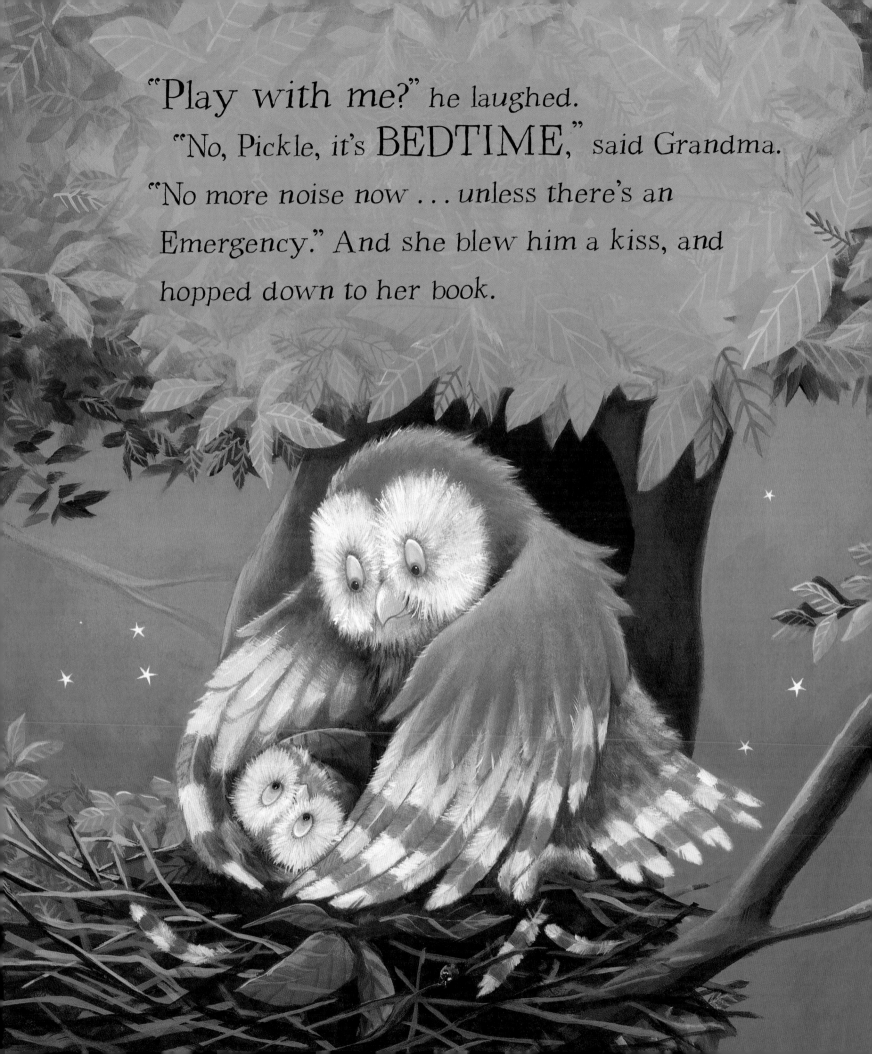

Grandma sat in the stillness.
All was quiet at last. She was
just about to start reading when ...

"GRANDMA, GRANDMA!
IT'S AN EMERGENCY!"

"IT'S AN EMERGENCY!"

thought Grandma. "Oh my goodness!"

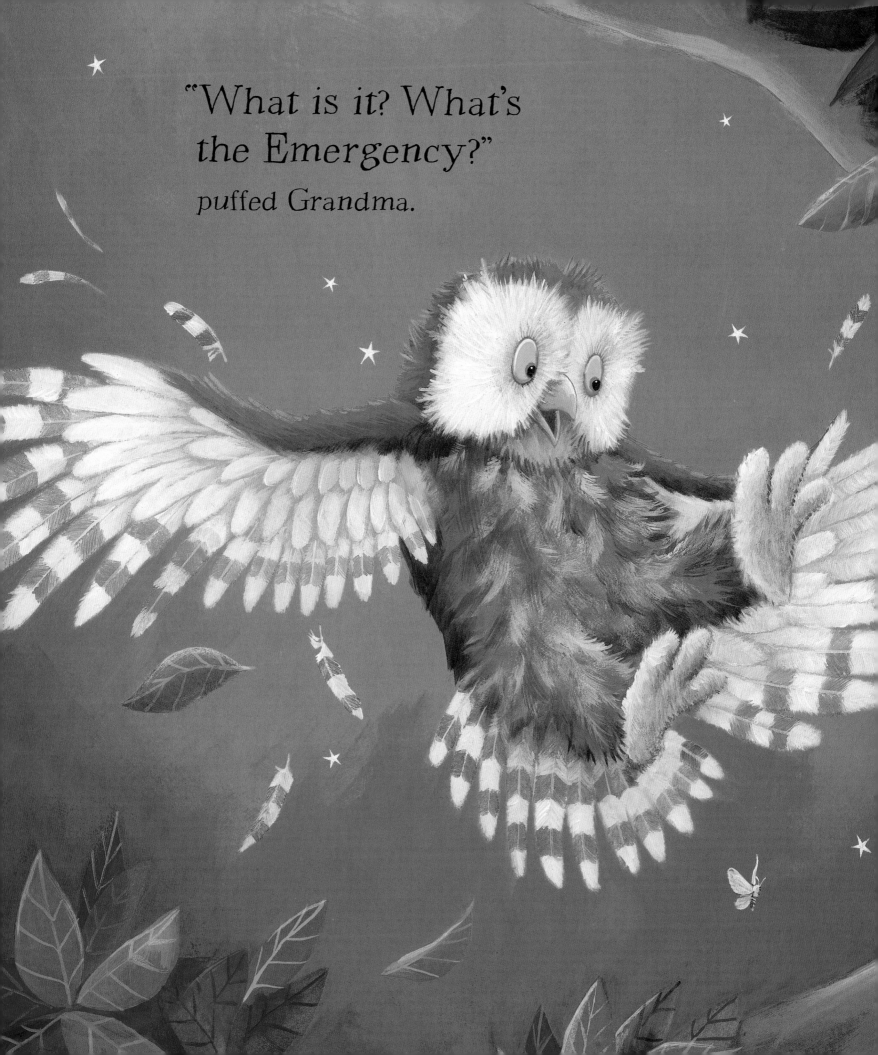

"What is it? What's the Emergency?" puffed Grandma.

"I'm not sleepy!" said Mo.
"I don't want to go to bed.
I want to play!"

Grandma squeezed into Mo's cosy nest next to him and cuddled him.

"The thing is, Mo, it's bedtime, and at bedtime SOMEONE has to go to bed," she said. "So, I have a very good idea. I'LL go to bed, and YOU can stay up!"

"YES! YES! YES!" laughed Mo,
"and you'll need fresh leaves ... and a
Bedtime Biscuit ... and tucking in
... and EVERY TIME I come up
I'll blow you a kiss."

Mo was very busy.
He didn't have time to play.
It was hard work putting
Grandma to bed.

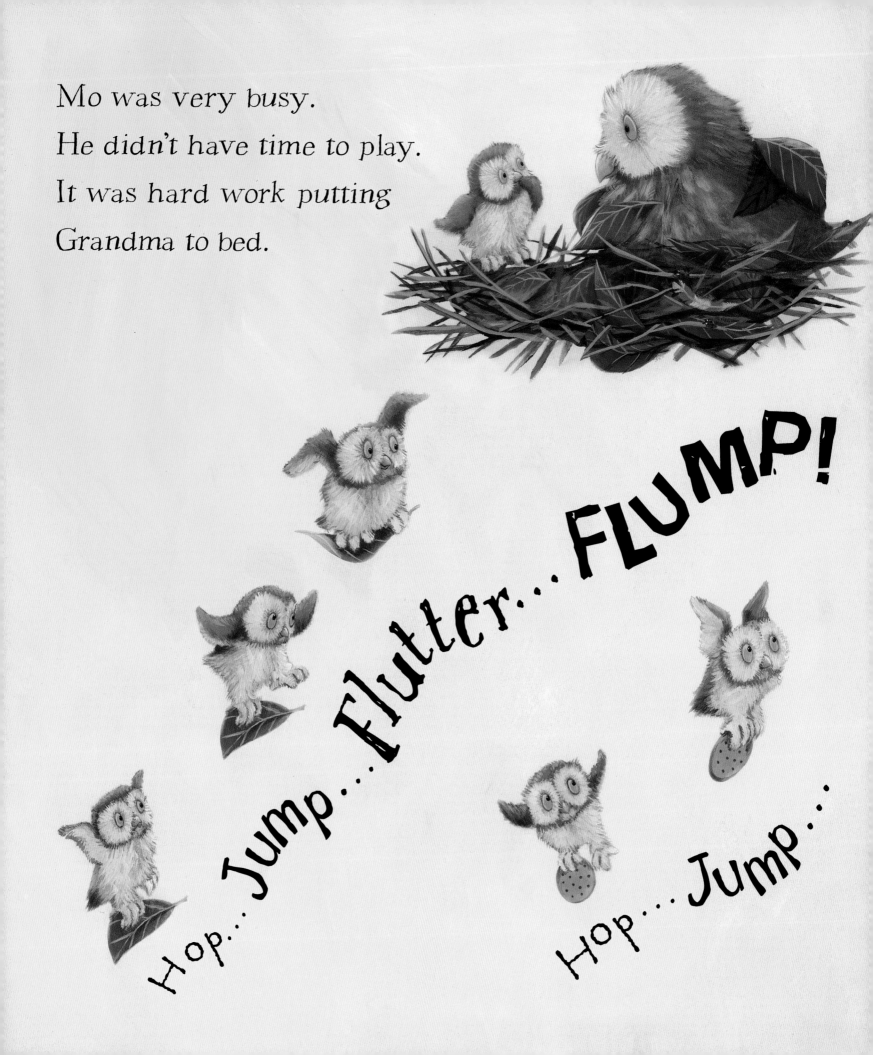

Hop... Jump... Flutter... FLUMP!

Hop... Jump...

Flutter . . . FLUMP!

Flutter . . . FLUMP!

Hop . . . Jump . . . Flutter . . . FLUMP!

Most of the stars were gone when a little voice called up from below. "Grandma? ...I'm really sleepy." "Of course you are, Poppet, it's very late!" said Grandma.

And she hopped down the
tree to her favourite owlet.
"On my back," she said.

Flutter...

to his nest...

Jump...

all the way up...

Hop...

Grandma carried Mo...

FLUMP!

at the top of the tree.

Grandma snuggled Mo down
and folded soft leaves over him.
"Time for bed," she smiled.
Then Grandma smoothed Mo's
feathers gently, blew him a kiss
and hopped back down
the tree to her book.

More fabulous books from Little Tiger Press!

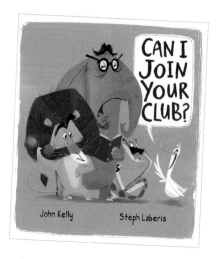

For information regarding any of the above books or for our catalogue, please contact us:
Little Tiger Press Ltd, 1 Coda Studios, 189 Munster Road, London SW6 6AW
Tel: 020 7385 6333 • E-mail: contact@littletiger.co.uk • www.littletiger.co.uk